First published 1985 by
Walker Books Ltd
184-192 Drummond Street
London NW1 3HP

First printed 1985
Printed and bound by L.E.G.O., Vicenza, Italy

British Library Cataloguing in Publication Data
Lloyd, David, *1945-*
Silly games. —(Dinosaur days)
I. Title II. Cross, Peter III. Series
823′.914[J] PZ7

ISBN 0-7445-0299-3

Tessa Lyle.

SILLY GAMES

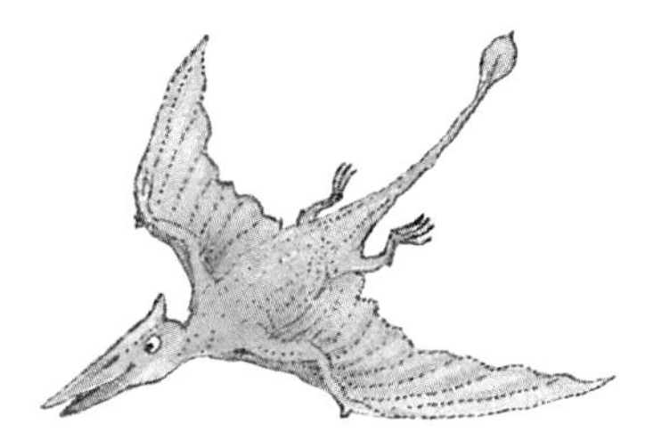

Written by David Lloyd
Illustrated by Peter Cross

WALKER BOOKS
LONDON

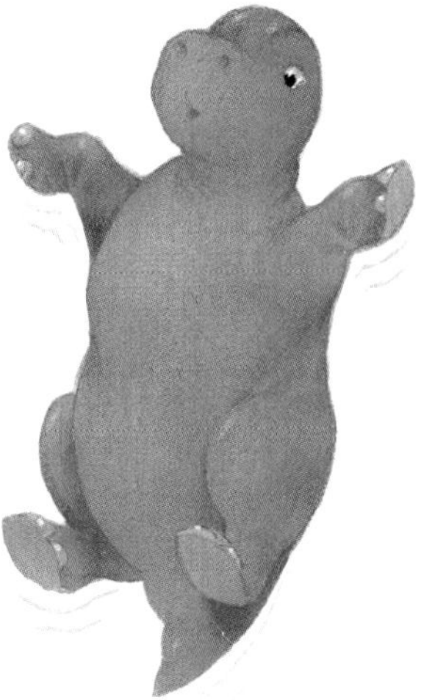

Little So-and-So
was being silly.

Jumpetty

Jumpetty

Jump

He bounced on
So-So-Slowly's tummy.

So-So-Slowly
rolled over.
Little So-and-So
danced onto her nose.

hoppity
hoppity
hop

ooooo

So-So-Slowly stood up.

oooooooooooooooooooO

It was a long, long way
to the ground.

So-So-Slowly strode across the world.

Little So-and-So raced and chased around her feet.

ohhhhhhhhhhhh

They saw Atlas,
the giant mountain turtle.

ahhhhhhhhhhh

They saw
little Eohippus.

They came to
the water-hole.

Gurgle Slurp

The dinosaurs
were drinking.

So-So-Slowly sucked in
gallons of water.

shoooWhhh

Her cheeks were
green balloons.

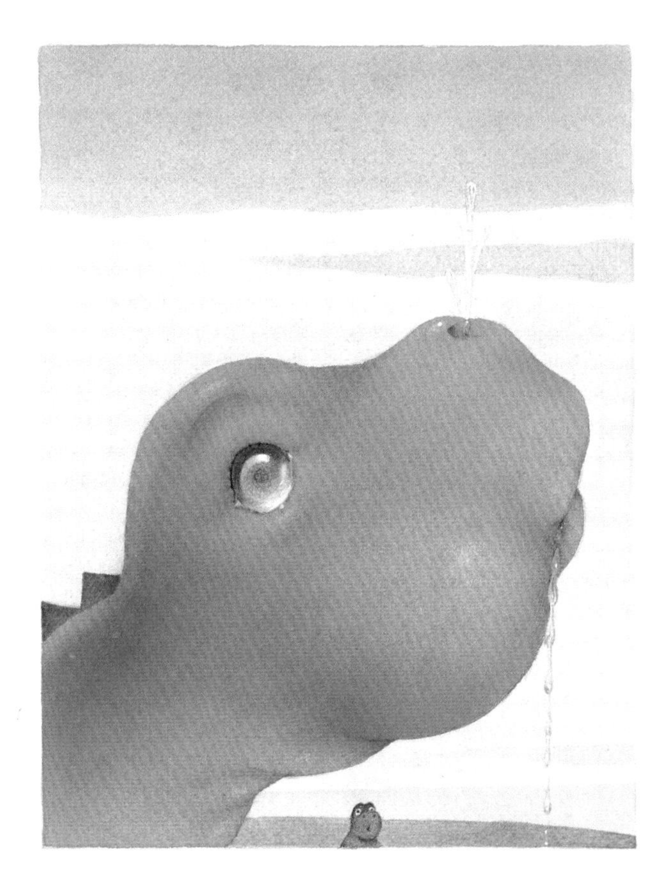

So-So-Slowly blew
out the water,
just for fun.

whooshhhhhhh

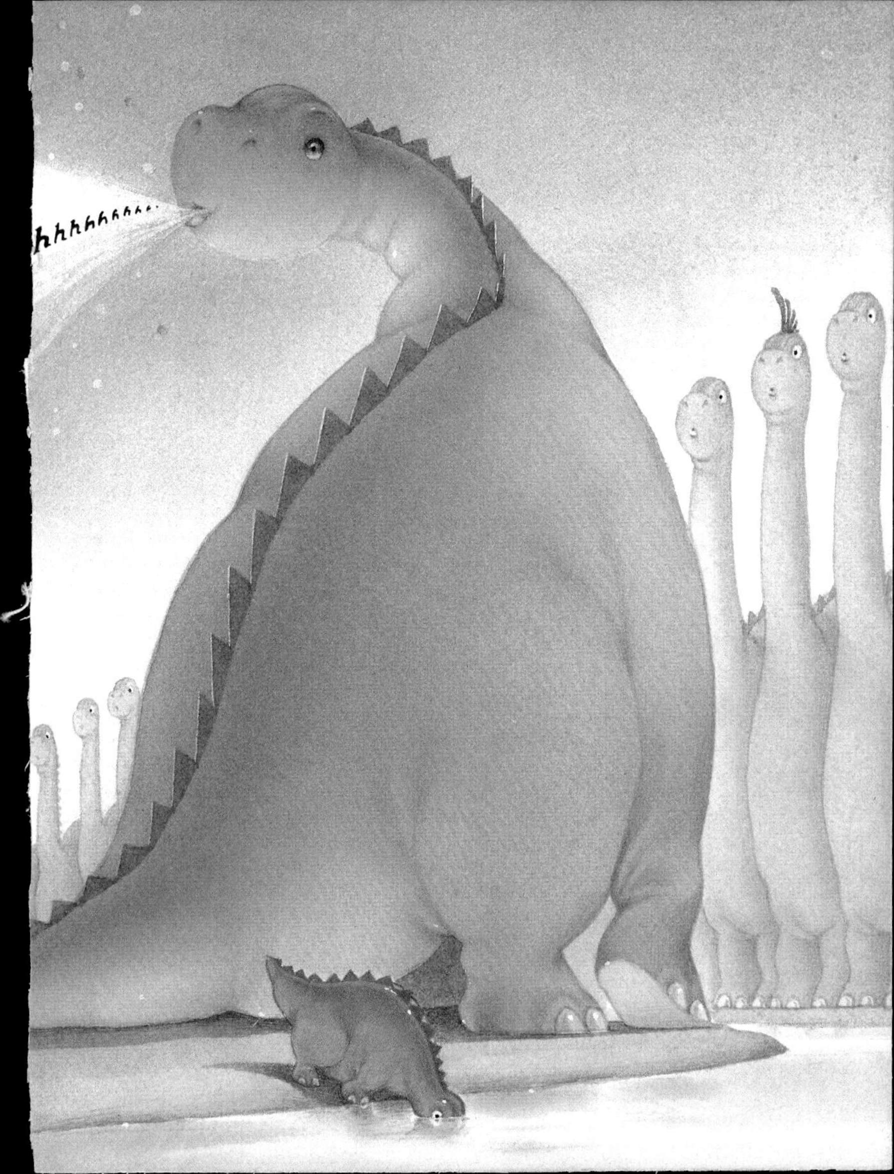
hhhhhhhh..

Little So-and-So
blew water
at High-and-Mighty.

hmph
High-and-Mighty
was not
amused.

So-So-Slowly took
Little So-and-So away.

The last rays of the sun
shone softly
on the dinosaurs.

Good night, So-So-Slowly.
Good night, Little So-and-So.
It's time to sleep.